Leap of Faith

by Bernadette Kelly

STONE ARCH BOOKS
a capstone imprint

First published in the United States in 2010
by Stone Arch Books
A Capstone Imprint
151 Good Counsel Drive, P.O. Box 669
Mankato, Minnesota 56002
www.capstonepub.com

First published in Australia by Black Dog Books in 2006

Copyright © Bernadette Kelly 2006

Library of Congress Cataloging-in-Publication Data is available on the Library of
Congress website.

Library Binding: 978-1-4342-1932-9

Art Director: Kay Fraser
Graphic Designer: Emily Harris
Production Specialist: Michelle Biedscheid
Photo Credit: Capstone Studio/Karon Dubke, cover

Leap
of
Faith

by Bernadette Kelly

"So who is this Penelope O'Reilly person, anyway?" I asked, shifting impatiently in my saddle.

"You'll find out in a minute, Annie. You'd be finding out now if gear check hadn't taken so long," Austin Ryan complained. His tall, brown thoroughbred mare, Cruise, pawed at the ground.

Beside him, on my own horse, Bobby, I shrugged my shoulders. "I thought gear check was for safety," I said.

Reese Moriarty butted in. "It is for safety. Don't listen to Austin, Annie. He's just impatient to get to Penelope's lesson." Then Reese turned her attention to Austin. "Austin, skipping gear check wouldn't have made the clock go any faster, you know," she said, smoothing down her horse's messy gray mane. "Jefferson appreciates it, don't you, boy?"

The riding club gear check was when tack was checked for anything that could be dangerous, such as loose stitching or cracked leather that could break, or gear that didn't fit right, which could hurt our horses.

Once all the horses were checked, we were given the all-clear. Then we headed toward the riding club's jumping arena for the day's first lesson. Matt Snyder and Jessica Coulson made up the rest of the group.

Matt sat easily on his horse, Bullet, and Jessica rode her elegant little show horse.

Jessica's horse was named Ripple (although whenever she had the chance, Jessica liked to remind everyone that the mare's full show name was Ripponlea Duchess).

I'd only been a riding club member for a little while. I was still getting to know everybody. This was the first time I had heard Austin complain about anything. He did get a little intense sometimes, but that was just Austin.

Most of the time he ignored the rest of us, preferring to stay focused on his riding.

I knew that Austin had real ambitions. He wanted to ride in the Olympics one day. From what I had seen of Austin's riding, he'd probably make it.

Watching Austin clear the impossibly high jumps with Cruise always gave me confidence. It made me believe that if we worked hard and kept training, Bobby and I could someday make it over the much lower jumps that challenged me.

Reese pointed. "There's Penelope," she said. "Come on, let's get over there and get started."

I smiled. It seemed like Reese was just as excited to start the lesson as Austin was.

Reese explained that Penelope O'Reilly was the club's guest instructor for the day. Penelope was an international event rider who had ridden at tons of top courses around the world. In fact, Reese said, she had even won a medal at the world championships.

Penelope was in demand as a horse trainer and had her pick of the best horses to ride. For a world-class event rider to be teaching at a small country riding club like Ridgeview was a big deal.

We reined our horses to a stop and waited together for Penelope to start the lesson. She didn't seem to be in much of a hurry. Tall and thin, with long dark hair tied back in a ponytail, she stood on the side of the arena, having a conversation with Mr. Snyder, Matt's dad.

The horses were becoming unsettled, as if sensing our eagerness. Cruise had broken out in a nervous sweat, while Reese's gray horse, Jefferson, snorted and pawed the ground.

Ripple refused to stand still and Matt's horse, Bullet, danced on his hind legs — not that Matt seemed to mind much. Only Bobby stood still and calm.

I wasn't sure whether to be grateful for my well-behaved horse or disappointed that he wasn't showing more spirit.

After what seemed like forever, Penelope finished her conversation and wandered across the sandy ground to us.

I wondered what Penelope had planned for the lesson. Jumping — and for that matter, riding in general — was still new to me, but I couldn't think of anywhere I'd rather be than there, learning to improve my riding skills with every lesson.

It seemed unbelievable that not so long ago I had lived in the city. Back then, a fun day out was a trip to the mall with my friends. But ever since my father had accepted a job selling real estate in Ridgeview, my life had turned upside down.

Instead of a city apartment, I lived in the country. Instead of waking up to noisy traffic sounds every morning, my days began with chattering birds and the bleating of my father's sheep. I hung out with Reese, my next-door neighbor, whose life revolved around horses, instead of my old best friend, Jade, whose life revolved around fashion and shopping. Everything was different.

But the best change of all had been the arrival of my horse, Bobby.

My parents — well, my father, really — hadn't wanted me to have a horse. But Bobby and I had found each other when a neighbor, Mrs. Cameron, gave him to me.

So now I was a riding club member. If that wasn't enough to keep me busy, I had also landed a job at the local riding stables. The stables' owner, Erica, was a regular instructor at the riding club.

Erica was a tough boss, but she was an excellent instructor. I was learning plenty about horses and riding from her.

We were used to our regular instructors starting lessons right away, but the first thing Penelope did was direct us all into a circle around her. "First of all," she began, "how many of you are serious about your riding?"

All five of us shot our hands into the air.

Penelope nodded her approval. "Great. You're the riders of the future, and my job is to help you to achieve your goals. How many of you have ridden in a competition?"

This time only four hands went up. Penelope turned to Jessica first. "At what level do you compete?" she asked.

"I've ridden at shows. In the height and age classes," Jessica bragged.

Penelope didn't seem to be interested in shows. With an impatient wave of her hand, she asked, "But what about eventing?"

Jessica's face flushed. "Oh. Well, Mrs. Mason, our District Commissioner, said I could start at D rating. I haven't actually done any horse trials yet, but I'm planning on doing a lot of them — just as soon as the show season's over, of course."

There were a few smirks from the boys when Jessica mentioned how much she liked the show season. Neither of them had much time for "showies " like Jessica.

The instructor didn't comment. She just turned to Matt and waited for him to speak.

"Mostly I compete at games," he said proudly, "but I just got to the C rating for eventing."

Penelope nodded. "And you?" she asked Reese.

"I'm in training too," Reese told her. "But there aren't very many horse trials locally, so I've only competed at a couple of places. Mom doesn't like to drive too far for events."

Before Penelope could respond to Reese, Austin piped up. "I've done a lot of events," he said. "Eventing is the reason I ride. I'm rated B, but I want to get to A rating soon."

I shot Austin an admiring look. The highest riding-club level was A rating. I had seen A-rating jumps set up for the senior riders and they looked enormous. It seemed impossible that a horse and rider could jump so high.

If any one of us could make it to that level, I thought, *it would be Austin.*

Penelope brightened. "Ah," she said. "So you have goals. That's good. I will be interested to see what you can show me."

Penelope finally turned her attention to me. "And what about you?" she asked.

I didn't know what to say. I opened my mouth and nothing came out. Then I looked down at my saddle with embarrassment.

"She's just a beginner," Jessica said rudely.

Penelope turned, ignoring Jessica, and looked pointedly at me for an answer.

"Well, actually, I haven't really competed," I answered.

Penelope frowned. "Why not? Don't you want to?"

"No, it isn't that," I said. "I haven't been riding long, and I was just rated — on the same day as Jessica, actually."

I shot a sidelong glance at Jessica. I saw, with a tiny spike of satisfaction, that Jessica looked uncomfortable. I knew Jessica thought she was a much better rider than me. She hated being put into the same category as Bobby and me.

I had surprised everyone, especially myself, when I passed the rating test. Both Jessica and I had tried out for D rating, which meant that we had to walk, trot, and canter to Mrs. Mason's satisfaction. Then we had to jump a course of jumps set at 18 inches high.

I remembered the day clearly. I had passed each test with Jessica, even though I hadn't been a riding club member as long as she had. It had been an amazing experience.

Penelope smiled. "Well, don't worry," she said kindly. "We'll just have to get you started."

The horses had quieted, except for Bullet. He would settle for a minute or two and then suddenly start pawing at the ground, sending small chunks of grass and dirt flying. Matt patted Bullet's neck to calm him, while still listening carefully to what the instructor was saying.

Penelope continued. "Willowvale Riding Club is hosting a horse trial in a few weeks," she told us. "The entry forms are in the cafeteria area. I'd like you all to think about entering."

"I already entered!" Austin announced. "I sent my form in last week."

"Good," said Penelope. "There's nothing like getting out there and competing to help you along with your riding."

Suddenly her tone changed and became businesslike. "Okay, let's see what you can do," she announced. She placed her hands on her hips and snapped, "Get those horses moving."

The lesson had begun.

Chapter
Two

Penelope stood in the middle of the arena and asked us to begin with a brief warm-up. She told us to trot, then canter our horses around the ring. Her voice boomed constantly. We had to concentrate hard to keep up with her directions.

"Rhythm is most the important thing," she shouted. "Whatever pace you and your horse are traveling at, it must have rhythm. Don't be pulling on the reins, speeding up and slowing down all the time. Show your horse the pace you want, and then let him do it. Don't be constantly bothering him. This means you should have a steady seat. You should not be relying on your hands and reins for balance."

I struggled to keep up with the instructions. I would try to concentrate on a command, like heels down, shoulders back. But before my brain could finish that thought, Penelope had moved on, and I found myself two steps behind the rest of the group. A few times I turned the wrong way and had to re-join the line. I could feel my face burning. I hoped it wasn't as red as it felt.

Penelope began dragging trotting poles from a stack on the edge of the arena while she called out instructions.

Once she had six poles laid out on the ground in a parallel grid, she instructed us to take our horses over them. "Remember to keep your rhythm," Penelope called. "Don't slow down or speed up over the poles. Keep a safe distance. I don't want to see you within kicking distance of the horse in front."

One after another, everyone rode through the poles. Penelope moved a couple of jump standards — the stands that held the rails in place — onto the ends of the poles. She kept shouting directions the whole time.

She lifted the first two poles into position on the wing, so that they formed a crossbar hurdle. The next time we went through the grid, the horses would have to leap instead of step over the last pole.

When Ripple reached the crossbar, she hesitated.

I could tell that Penelope had thought that might happen, because she yelled at Jessica, "Use your legs, Jessica. Your horse cannot stop!"

Frowning, Jessica kicked hard at Ripple's sides. Ripple just kept going, up and over the jump.

Jessica looked pleased with herself. She headed back and took her place in the line.

Reese and Jefferson sailed through the course with no trouble. I had hoped to watch my inspiration, Austin, sail over the jump first. Instead, he held back, forcing me to go forward. I clung fiercely to Bobby's mane as he cleared the course.

"Annie!" Penelope yelled. "It's okay to grab his mane, but for heaven's sake, look up! If you stare at the ground, you'll end up there."

I jerked my head up nervously. I'd already ended up on the ground more than a few times in my short riding career.

Matt and Bullet went over fine, but Penelope yelled at Matt after he was done.

She said that he'd let his horse travel too fast. "You won't get anywhere by traveling too fast," she told him. "This kind of jumping exercise is designed to help your horse with his balance and coordination. Racing through will only put him at risk of making a mistake and hurting himself."

I looked over at Matt. He looked a little embarrassed. I knew that Matt and Bullet loved to race — that was why they were so good at the mounted games. But anyone could see that Matt really loved his horse, and he would never knowingly put Bullet at risk of an injury.

Before Austin entered the grid, Penelope raised the poles. Now the jumps were quite high. Austin cantered in confidently and Cruise sailed smoothly over the first bars. But as horse and rider prepared to take off over the final obstacle in the row, a plastic bag appeared from nowhere.

Pushed by the slightest of breezes, it bounced and waved across the course at exactly the wrong moment.

Cruise spooked and darted sharply to the left, sideswiping the jump and unseating Austin. For one long moment, Austin clung desperately to the saddle as he slipped down the side of the horse. He dangled, then met the ground shoulder first. Cruise stopped sharply. Austin lay still for a moment before scrambling to his feet.

"Are you okay?" Penelope asked. She fixed the jump standard as Austin grabbed his horse's reins.

Austin, red-faced and shaken, answered, "I'm fine."

But he didn't seem fine at all. Without another word, he marched off toward the parking lot, pulling his horse along beside him.

Shocked, we all stared after him. No one said anything for a moment.

"Is that it?" asked Reese. "He's not even going to try again?"

Penelope sighed as she watched Austin leave. She checked her watch and then announced that the lesson was over.

After a dressage lesson with Erica, it was time for lunch.

Austin and Cruise were nowhere to be seen. All the girls could talk about was what had happened during Penelope's lesson.

"Serves him right," said Jessica. "He's always showing off anyway."

"That's totally unfair," Reese said. "Just because Austin is a better rider than the rest of us doesn't make him a show-off. He practices all the time. That's what gives him an edge."

Jessica snorted. "Well, we didn't see too much edge today," she said, tossing her hair back.

"What happened to him?" I wondered out loud. "He didn't look hurt. I thought you were supposed to get back on after you fall off a horse."

Reese sighed. "I don't know," she said. "He was really, really excited to have a lesson with Penelope. She's, like, one of his heroes. Austin doesn't ride for fun like the rest of us do. He wants to make it to the top."

"Well, after today, he's going to need some luck," said Jessica nastily.

* * *

Later, when Reese and I were getting ready to go home, Reese wanted to talk about Penelope's suggestion that each of us should enter the horse trials. "I know that event,"

Reese said. "Willowvale's not far away. We did it last year and had a great day. Mom won't mind taking me to that one. What about you, Annie? Do you think you'll enter?"

"A competition?" I replied quietly as I brushed Bobby's hair. "I don't know, Reese. I just don't know if I'm ready."

But Reese was already making plans for the day as she threw a blanket over Jefferson's broad back. She ignored my doubtful tone.

"Of course you are. You may as well get started. Besides . . . " Reese grinned, her eyes full of mischief. "I bet Jessica's going."

I frowned. "That's sneaky," I accused my friend.

"Yep," said Reese happily.

I laughed. But inside, I was thinking that there was no way Reese could be serious about me entering the horse trials.

There was no way I was ready. The thought of riding in any competition was just too terrifying, especially after Austin's fall that morning.

Austin was an experienced rider. If he could fall off during a lesson, what trouble could I, a beginner, get myself into at a competition?

"It's done," Reese said happily. "Mom sent in the entry form for the one-day event with both of our names on it."

Reese sat cross-legged on the grassy school lawn, using our lunch break to soak up some of the sun's warmth. We'd only been back at school for a week. There would be plenty of warm days to go.

I had adjusted well to life in Ridgeview over summer vacation. I already knew Reese, who was in the same grade, and I'd crossed paths with Matt and Laura Snyder in the halls a couple of times. They always waved and said hi to me.

Seeing some familiar faces meant that being at a new school hadn't been as scary as it could have been. So far things were okay. The teachers were nice. So were my classmates, although I'd mostly been hanging out with Reese's friends.

Today, it was just the two of us. The others were all trying out for the school basketball team. I used to play basketball at my old school, but now, all I wanted to do was ride horses.

It hadn't even been too bad having my mother, a teacher, working at my school. I didn't think anyone had figured out yet that my mom was a math and science teacher at Ridgeview High School.

Most of the time, Mom was too busy to keep tabs on me. We drove to school together, but we parted every morning in the teachers' parking lot and met again each afternoon after the bell.

At first, I had been really self-conscious in my new school uniform. In fact, I really hated it. I was used to wearing a uniform. But at my old school the uniform had been a simple pale blue sweater, white shirt, and casual black pants, with skirts for hotter days. Everyone had worn sneakers, and teachers didn't care that much if you wore accessories or left your shirt untucked.

Ridgeview High was much stricter about dress code. The school colors were red, white, and charcoal gray. The girls' winter uniform was a gray wool dress. Sneakers were only allowed during gym class, and jewelry was a definite no-no.

I didn't like it at first. It took me several days, but after a while, I got used to it. Everyone looked the same, so I stopped worrying about it. By now, I didn't even think about it.

Austin Ryan and Jessica Coulson attended a different school over an hour's bus ride away. That was just fine with me. I liked Austin, but Jessica was not my favorite person. As it was, I found her hard enough to put up with at riding club.

I had been lying on my back with my eyes closed when Reese poked me in the arm.

"Did you hear what I said?" Reese asked. "About the horse trials."

I propped myself up on one elbow and turned to look at Reese with alarm.

"The horse trials? Well — it's just that I'm still not sure —"

"Too late for arguments," said Reese. "You're coming. Mom said Bobby could ride in our trailer with Jefferson."

Fear stabbed my chest. I didn't know a thing about horse competitions, least of all a one-day event. I was flattered that Reese wanted me to go and even more flattered that she thought I was a good enough rider to compete. And it was very kind of Mrs. Moriarty to offer to take Bobby. But there was no way I could accept.

I stared at Reese. How could I tell my friend I wasn't going when Reese was so excited about the arrangements she'd made?

* * *

After school that night, Mom met me in the parking lot as usual, but she didn't have her bag and keys. "Sorry, honey. We have a staff meeting, and I forgot all about it," Mom explained. "It shouldn't take very long. Why don't you wait for me in the library?"

When I entered the library, it was empty except for Mrs. Bensted, the librarian. She had her head bent over some files and didn't even see me come in.

I had planned to catch up on some English homework, but when I saw a computer, I had a better idea.

I knew I wouldn't be riding at Willowvale, but I could still go along to watch and to keep Reese happy. And there was no point watching if I didn't have a clue what was happening.

From conversations I'd overheard at riding club, I had picked up some information about horse trials. I knew that the horse trials consisted of a dressage test, a show-jumping round, and a cross-country round. But I didn't know what any of that actually meant.

I was sure the others were already sick of my endless questions. Maybe I could find some answers on the Internet.

I Googled "horse trials." A long list of links flashed up on the screen, but the one that caught my eye was a riding club information site. I clicked on the link and waited while it loaded.

When the page flickered up on the screen, I was thrilled. It was exactly what I needed. It had information about all the different events, rules and regulations, tips for safe riding, and even photos of riders from various clubs all over the country.

I leaned forward to read the screen. This was like opening a door into another world and finding the answers to all of my questions.

I clicked on the link for one-day event rules and then printed the information.

Mrs. Bensted looked up briefly as the printer fired into action and paper began feeding through. I read the screen while I waited for the paper copy.

A horse trial is a competition with three separate phases. The first phase is dressage, the second phase is cross-country, and the final phase is show jumping. In the dressage phase, you are required to ride a test.

I scanned the screen and found a link for dressage tests. There were several different tests for each level. I selected a couple of different tests for D rating.

They showed a page with a list of numbered instructions. Beside each instruction was a blank space for the judge to write in a comment and another space for a numbered mark from zero to ten. I read the first instruction.

Trot in at A.

Huh? I thought. *What in the world does that mean?*

As I read on, I realized that the arena must have lettered markers set out around it. The letters were the same for each test. I looked around the site until I found a dressage arena map.

It looks complicated, I thought. *What have I gotten myself into?*

I used the computer mouse to switch between reading the instructions on the test and looking at the map.

I sighed deeply. The printer stopped. I printed the map and the dressage test before retrieving the whole stack, a thick wad of printed pages. I decided I would take them home and read them carefully. Maybe that would make things clearer.

Chapter Four

I could always tell who had cooked dinner in my household by the way it was served.

My mother liked to serve everything in bowls in the middle of the table so that people could help themselves.

When my father cooked, he would serve food directly onto the plates, with each separate vegetable and piece of meat given its own little space. He hated it when things on the plate touched.

Sometimes I cooked dinner. I always made stirfry. I loved the way the bright ingredients were all thrown in together and tossed around — a messy madness of color, flavor, and texture.

Tonight was obviously Dad's night. I stared down at my plate. Roasted chicken with steamed broccoli, carrots, and potatoes. Each type of food had a clean sliver of white plate showing between it and the next.

Mom took a large pitcher from the fridge and began pouring water into three skinny glasses. She placed them onto the table one by one.

"Willowvale Riding Club is holding a one-day horse trial," I announced casually.

The water splashed the insides of my glass as it filled. Then Mom put the pitcher onto the counter.

"Hmm. That sounds dangerous," said Mom, frowning. "What would you have to do?"

I knew Mom worried a lot about my safety since I'd started riding. *She shouldn't worry*, I thought.

"Oh, there's a dressage test to memorize," I said, trying to act like I knew exactly what would happen. "Then there's a show-jumping round and a cross-country round. I'm rated D. But I'm actually not planning —"

I was about to explain that I wouldn't be riding when Dad cut in.

"And how much does this cost?" he demanded.

I puffed out my cheeks in frustration. Dad was always ruining things by asking about money.

"I don't know. Not much," I told him uncertainly.

"Willowvale, huh?" Dad scratched his chin and looked thoughtful. "MC Developments is looking to develop a property in Willowvale. I believe the manager has a daughter who belongs to a riding club."

"Really?" I said brightly. I wondered which riding club the daughter rode with. "You could come along and watch, Dad. Maybe your manager friend will be there."

"You're not going," he said.

I stared at him. As usual, he hadn't let me finish, and now he had things all wrong. Even if I had wanted to ride, he should have been more excited. I thought Dad would be happy that I was making friends and getting involved in my new community.

The minute my father said no, suddenly, more than anything, I wanted to ride at the one-day event.

"Why not?" I asked.

"Annie, I said no," Dad said firmly.
"Besides, we don't have a horse trailer. There's
no way for that old donkey to get there."

I had been about to mention the Moriartys'
offer to take Bobby. Instead, I glared at my
father.

"He's not a donkey!" I yelled.

"That's enough. You're not going and
that's that." Dad began carefully arranging
vegetables on his fork, one piece at a time.

I left the table and stomped out of the
kitchen, leaving my half-eaten dinner. As I
headed to my room, I heard Mom say, "Rob,
that was a little harsh. Why on earth can't
she go? I'm sure we could get her horse there
somehow."

I stopped to hear Dad's answer. "Mark
is one of our biggest clients," he said. "He'll

probably be there to watch his daughter. The last thing I need is Annie embarrassing me on that old horse. She'd probably fall off or something."

I couldn't believe it. He didn't care about my safety at all. All he cared about was his stupid client! I ran into my bedroom and slammed the door so hard it rattled.

I lay on my bed and stared up at the ceiling. *That's it. He's not getting away with it*, I thought angrily.

I'm going to that event, I decided. *And he's not going to stop me.*

* * *

When I arrived at Erica's stables for work, there was a group lesson going on in the indoor arena. It was Reese, Jessica, and Matt. They were all practicing for the one-day horse trial.

I felt a stab of jealousy. Erica's time was precious, with other people's horses to train and paid lessons to give. Even though I worked at the stables, I would have had to pay full price for a private lesson. I just couldn't afford it. My parents had made it clear that I had to help with the cost of keeping Bobby and being in the riding club.

Besides, I was saving to buy new tack for Bobby. I had already managed to scrape enough money together for a new bridle, but then Bobby had gotten hurt and he'd needed shoes.

My hard-earned savings had been quickly swallowed up with that, even though my mom helped me out with the cost. Now I was starting all over again.

So far I had only the embarrassingly small amount of ten dollars. That was enough for about one-tenth of a bridle.

Still, I thought, *it would have been nice to have been asked to join the lesson.*

I hurried into the stables before the others could see me. I began cleaning the stalls the way Erica had taught me, making sure not to leave behind any soiled or wet straw.

My thoughts turned to the one-day event. Things had really gotten complicated. I had let Mrs. Moriarty and Reese believe I was going even though I wasn't planning on it. Now that Dad had forbidden me to go, I was definitely going, but my parents thought I wasn't. I was still furious with my father. As usual, he was only thinking about himself.

I could hear Erica shouting instructions to the three riders. "The judges are looking for horses that show obedience and calmness. They want to see you riding accurately to the markers. For C rating and above, they will want to see that you can trot on the correct diagonals and that your horse can lead with the correct leg in the canter. Jessica, even though you'll be riding in D rating, you might as well start learning this stuff."

"Ripple was trained for the show ring. She always canters on the correct lead," Jessica said.

Jessica sounds so smug sometimes, I thought. I had a feeling Jessica would be going to Willowvale with her father's approval — and probably a bunch of new gear, too.

I jabbed angrily at a pile of manure. It just wasn't fair.

Chapter Five

I heard Erica's voice again. "Everyone go large around the arena, and keep a good distance between each horse. I don't want anyone getting kicked."

I finished with the stalls and began sweeping the entryway. No more voices came from the direction of the arena, and I guessed that the lesson was over. The riders were leaving the arena when they spotted me.

"Annie!" Reese called.

I looked up and waved. Still carrying a broom, I walked down the hallway to meet them. They all looked pretty pleased with themselves.

Must have been a good lesson, I thought bitterly.

Matt and Reese rode up to me. Jessica hung back, frowning. I was getting used to Jessica's moods. I decided to ignore her.

"Annie! Where were you?" Reese asked me angrily.

I had no idea what she was talking about. "When?" I asked.

"I called to ask if you wanted to share the lesson," Reese said. "Your father said he'd tell you that I called."

"Oh!" I instantly felt better when the truth dawned on me. Reese, at least, had wanted to include me in the group. But then I realized what Reese was saying. A thread of panic wound its way across the inside of my stomach.

What had Reese said to my father? Even worse, what might have my father said to Reese?

I imagined the conversation. "No, Reese, Annie doesn't need a lesson. She's not going to the horse trials."

But if my father had said anything like that, Reese wasn't letting on.

"Well," Reese demanded again, "where were you? How come you never called me back, anyway?"

I shook my head and threw my hands in the air. "Not again," I said in an annoyed tone. "My dad is so busy. It's not the first time he's forgotten to give me a message. Mom's always yelling at him for it. I'm sorry. I didn't know anything about it."

Matt grinned at me. "We booked another one for the same time next week," he said. "Wanna join us for that one?"

I sighed, scuffing my foot lightly on the concrete floor of the hallway. "I can't," I said. "I have to work."

Jessica chose that moment to butt in. "It's probably better that way," she said with a concerned frown. "You wouldn't be able to keep up with us."

"You think so?" I replied irritably. "We'll see about that at the one-day event."

Jessica choked back a snort of laughter. "I guess we will," she retorted.

My words were confident, but inside I felt panicked.

For one thing, I had to get to the event. Then I had to compete without totally embarrassing myself.

The last thing I want to do is screw up and prove Jessica right, I thought.

I turned back to Matt and Reese. "Where's Austin?" I asked.

Matt shook his head. "Didn't want to come," he said. "He says he's not going to the event anyway, so there's no point."

"But he already signed up. I thought he loved eventing," I said.

Matt shrugged. "So did I. But that's what he said. If you want to know the truth, I think he might have kind of freaked out after falling off the other day."

That was not good. Matt's idea made me feel nervous.

"Maybe we should go and see him," I suggested timidly. "We could try to change his mind."

Matt and Reese looked at each other, then back at me.

"You don't know Austin," Reese said. "He can be pretty determined. And I know he won't want us to get involved. The best thing to do is leave him alone. He'll get over it — eventually."

I nodded, but I was worried. Austin was the best rider in the group. Why would he suddenly pull out of the horse trials? Was he afraid?

Maybe eventing was a lot more dangerous than I thought.

* * *

Austin didn't know it, but I was on a mission to get him to the horse trials. Ever since I joined the riding club, I had admired Austin's determination to succeed and his courage at being the only person in my group to tackle the highest jumps. *If Austin is afraid to compete,*

I thought, *then there must be something to be afraid of.*

Austin was my good-luck charm when it came to jumping. I knew that the only way I would have the courage to ride in the competition was if Austin rode too.

I was determined to ride because I needed to show my father he was wrong. But first, I would have to find a way to get Austin to change his mind.

I had thought about a few ways to make it happen. I could beg Austin to ride, but then he would definitely think I was a loser. I could tell him the truth, but I didn't think that he would compete just to make me feel better.

No. The only way to get what I wanted was to trick Austin into riding.

I came up with a plan. I would pretend to be a much worse rider than I actually was.

Austin, being such a perfectionist, would get frustrated and show me how to do it. Then he would realize that he really did want to ride after all and go to the event. It was just like a plot from a movie.

I had it all worked out.

* * *

I held the phone to my ear and listened anxiously to the ring on the other end. While I waited for someone to pick up, I wondered if I was about to make a terrible mistake.

I figured there were two possibilities. If my idea worked, Austin would ride at the horse trials. No one would have to know that I had anything to do with it.

If it didn't work, not only would Austin think I was a total loser, but so would Reese and the others. Especially since Reese had told me to leave Austin alone.

Luckily, I didn't have to think about it anymore, because a voice said, "Hello?"

"Hello, um . . . Austin? Is that you?" I asked.

"Who is this?" he asked.

"It's Annie. Annie Boyd. From the riding club."

"Annie?" Austin sounded confused. "Um . . . what's up?"

I could almost hear his brain trying to figure out what on earth I was calling for. I breathed deeply. Gripping the phone, I took a long, deep breath.

Finally, I spoke. "Austin, I was wondering if you would . . . I mean . . . I have a favor to ask."

"Okay, what is it?" A doubtful tone crept into Austin's voice.

I felt like shrinking into my shoes with embarrassment. I couldn't speak.

"So?" Austin asked. "What's up, Annie?"

Suddenly, I knew I was doing the wrong thing. Why had I ever thought this was a good idea? But it was too late. If I hung up now, he would think I was a loser and that I was totally crazy, too.

"Austin," I began again, "I was wondering if you would be willing to give me a jumping lesson." It was out. I gulped in a breath of air and waited.

"I thought you were working for Erica," he said, sounding confused. "Why don't you get a lesson from her?"

I had expected this question. "I was . . . I mean, I am," I said quickly.

I wasn't about to tell Austin that I couldn't afford to pay for a lesson with Erica or that I had another reason for asking him instead of Reese.

"She's really busy and can't fit me in," I lied. "It doesn't matter. I mean . . . it's okay if you don't want to."

Judging by the silence on the line, Austin was obviously trying to think of a way to say no. How could I get off the phone without embarrassing myself even more?

But when Austin spoke again, he just sounded a little confused. "You want me to give you a lesson?"

"Well," I said, "it's just that you're such a good rider, and I just started. I thought you might be able to give me a few tips to help me get better. You know, before the one-day event at Willowvale."

"Oh." Austin's voice went flat. "You're going to that?"

"Listen, it's okay —" I began, but Austin interrupted.

"Why don't you bring Bobby over here?" he suggested. "I live on Baker Road. I have an arena and jumps. What about tomorrow?"

I agreed. I held onto the phone long after Austin hung up, still wondering if I'd made the right decision.

Chapter Six

The ride to Austin's house was an easy one. Baker's Road was located just off the main road into Ridgeview, about a ten-minute horseback ride from Hillgrove.

Jessica Coulson lived on the same street. I had been there once to buy some secondhand tack for Bobby. I'd been embarrassed when I found out that it was Jessica's old tack.

When I turned Bobby into Austin's driveway, all I could see of the house was some red brick behind a thick row of shrubs and trees. The trees wound along the driveway right to the back of the house.

Beyond them, everything looked neat and clean. The grass was freshly mown. The fields were fenced with wood painted a crisp white. Everything looked lush and cared for.

There was a horse trailer parked beside a fancy-looking brick shed. I rode around it and abruptly came upon a sandy open-air riding arena that had been fenced all around with more white posts and rails.

A course of five colored show jumps had been set up in the arena. The jumps were at least three feet high, with a couple of spreads that looked even wider than that.

I swallowed back the lump of fear that lurched into my throat. Austin wouldn't expect me to jump those, would he? But then I laughed to myself. No way!

Austin appeared from behind the horse trailer. He nodded a greeting, his expression serious. Without a word, he pointed to the arena and headed toward it, leaving me to follow on Bobby.

Once Austin had led me and my horse onto the arena, he got straight to the point. He didn't sound at all friendly.

"Nobody has ever asked me to give a lesson before. I'm not really sure what you want me to teach you," he said.

"Oh," I said. I swallowed hard.

Come on! I told myself. Don't just sit there acting dumb, say something.

"I'm not very confident when I'm jumping," I told him. "I thought you might be able to just, you know, show me how you do it."

Austin stared at me doubtfully. "What do you mean?" he asked.

My mouth was dry, and I could suddenly feel a headache coming on. What on earth had I been thinking? This was a terrible idea. Any minute now Austin was going to see right through me and my ridiculous plan. And then what was I going to do?

As I struggled to think of an answer for Austin, a younger girl on a very small, very cute Shetland pony rode into the arena. I recognized her from the riding club. She rode in the junior group.

"Natalie, get lost. Can't you see I'm busy here?" Austin snapped at the little girl.

Natalie ignored him and looked at me. "I know you!" she said.

I grinned. Natalie had a sweet face. I liked the way she completely ignored Austin.

"And I know you," I said. "Are you Austin's little sister?"

Natalie nodded sadly, as if that was the worst possible thing to be.

"What's your horse's name?" Natalie asked me.

Abruptly, Austin interrupted. "It's Bobby. Now come on, Nat, get out of here. Take Cheeky back to the stable. We're about to start a lesson."

The little girl's eyes widened with eagerness. "Can I watch?" she asked.

I could see that Austin was about to say no. "I don't mind," I said. "Natalie's probably a better rider than me anyway!"

Austin hesitated. Then he rolled his eyes. "Put Cheeky away first," he said. "Then you can watch."

Natalie happily trotted off toward the stable. "I'll be right back," she called over her shoulder.

Austin started me off jumping over very small crossbars. He was really bossy.

I tried to stop the anger that was already bubbling inside me. I'd thought I was going to help Austin, and here he was bossing me around like I was a five-year-old. I felt a stab of sympathy for Natalie. It would be awful to have to deal with Austin's moods every single day of your life!

Austin gave me instructions in a boring, stiff way. He told me that I needed to think about my seat and hands when I jumped. My hands on the reins should be held still, not pulling back as the horse went over each obstacle. My seat should be steady, he told me, not bumping around and unbalancing the horse.

I rode around the arena, listening to Austin's instructions and trying to ride the way he told me. Bobby plodded over the crossbars patiently, but I found it incredibly difficult to keep my hands still. And I was definitely bumping around in the saddle — a lot.

I had planned to pretend to ride badly, but it turned out that I didn't have to pretend. Judging by Austin's impatient growl, he obviously thought I was a horrible rider anyway. It didn't take him long to lose patience.

"You're grabbing him in the mouth," he yelled. "It's a miracle he'll jump for you at all when you treat him that way."

"I'm sorry," I said, wondering why on earth I'd set myself up for this. "I'm trying. It's just that there's so much to think about. It's all so hard!"

I felt tears threaten to spill down my cheeks. But there was no way I'd let Austin Ryan see me cry.

Natalie came wandering back and found
a shady spot under a tree at the edge of the
arena. Austin didn't even say anything when
his sister returned. He just kept repeating his
commands like a robot.

I was becoming more and more upset. The
instructors at riding club were never this mean.
It was like Austin didn't even care that I was
still a beginner. The angrier he became, the
worse I rode.

"What's wrong with you?" he finally shouted angrily. "Can't you follow a simple direction?"

"What's wrong with you?" I snapped back. I reined Bobby to a stop and added, "You're being so rude!"

Austin raised his eyebrows and snapped, "You wanted this lesson, remember?"

"Yes, I did. But I didn't think you'd be such a know-it-all," I yelled back.

Natalie joined the argument, taking my side. "Yeah, Austin. You're such a bully. Why do you always have to be so mean?"

Austin turned his attention to Nat. "You stay out of this."

I turned to stare at Natalie too. I was furious with Austin and with myself. If it hadn't been for my stupid, stupid idea, none of this would be happening. I admired the little girl's attitude. She certainly wasn't about to let her older brother boss her around.

Then Natalie dropped her bombshell. "Well, I'm not the one who's afraid to ride my horse," she yelled at her brother.

Austin glared at her. "I'm not afraid, Natalie," he growled angrily. "Just mind your own business."

"Oh yeah?" Natalie replied. "If you're not afraid, then how come you haven't ridden Cruise since you got home from the riding club the other day? And if you're not afraid, how come you told Matt you were skipping the Willowvale event?"

Natalie turned to me. "He even told Mom he was thinking about giving up riding altogether," she said quietly, as if she were telling a secret. "Why would he do that if he wasn't scared of riding?"

I was beginning to feel more than a little uncomfortable, and not just because I seemed to be caught in the middle of a fight between Natalie and Austin.

I suddenly knew why this whole thing with Austin was bothering me. He was so far ahead of me. If Austin was afraid, he must think there was something to be afraid of. Jumping was fun. But it could be risky too.

I wondered, not for the first time, if I was crazy to have let Reese talk me into riding at the horse trials. I wasn't experienced enough.

I knew I could still back out. Maybe I would.

"I'm not scared. It's just . . . " Austin stopped himself mid-sentence. He waved Natalie away with his arms. "Get lost. Go. You don't know what you're talking about."

Natalie took the hint and marched away, but not before she took a final parting shot.

"Prove it then, if you're not afraid," she told her brother. "Why don't you go and get Cruise right now and show Annie how you do it, instead of yelling at her all the time."

"I don't have to prove anything," Austin yelled back.

Both of them seemed to have forgotten all about me. I gently cleared my throat. Austin's eyes swung away from Natalie and back to me.

"Maybe I should go," I said awkwardly.

Austin hesitated. His face looked thoughtful, as if he was struggling with something.

Finally he said, "No, don't." All of the bossiness was gone from his voice. He sounded as if he really did want me to stay.

"I'll go get Cruise," he said. "My sister's a pain, but maybe it's not a bad idea to show you what I want you to do. Wait here. Just

ride around or something. I'll be right back."
Austin raced off to get his horse.

I watched him leave. *Well, this is an interesting turn of events*, I thought.

While Austin was gone, I decided to take the opportunity to practice riding over the jumps. I soon got really into it. Trotting around and over the little jumps was fun when there was nobody yelling at you.

Then, suddenly, I heard a voice calling to me. "Hey, that's more like it. Why didn't you ride like that before?" Austin had returned, riding Cruise.

Cruise fidgeted and refused to stand still while Austin leaned down to open the arena gate. I watched with admiration as Austin easily held the reins in one hand and stayed balanced, even though he was leaning far out of the saddle.

Austin rode up beside me. "You know, you ride better when you think nobody's watching," he told me.

My eyes widened. "I do?" I said.

"You do," Austin said. "Most people do when they're more relaxed. Maybe you were trying too hard before."

I nodded shyly. *I guess that makes sense*, I thought.

Austin went on to prove that relaxing was the key. He asked me to watch his position and follow him over the jump course. Almost immediately, it was easier for me to see what he'd been talking about.

I watched and copied exactly what Austin did. He leaned forward, up and out of the saddle. Then he allowed his hands to slide forward at the same moment that Cruise's front legs left the ground. That left the horse free to complete the leap without its rider getting in the way.

After a few rounds, Austin ended the lesson.

"That was a big improvement," he told me. "Good luck at Willowvale."

"I guess I'll see you there?" I asked. I didn't want to give away that I knew about him wanting to skip the event.

Austin didn't say anything. As I turned Bobby for home, I noticed that Austin was carefully studying the jumps in the arena. I wondered if he was thinking about lifting the jumps higher and trying them himself.

I wasn't brave enough to ask.

"Okay, everyone off your horses," Erica said, clapping her hands. It was the last lesson of the day at the riding club, and my last chance to polish my riding skills before the horse trials. But now Erica was telling us to dismount before we even started.

"What's this?" I asked Erica as a sheet of paper was pushed into my hand.

"It's a copy of your dressage test," Erica told me. "Read it over and memorize it. Then I'll give you all a chance to ride it through. Matt and Reese, you each have the same C rating test. Jessica and Annie, you two have identical D rating tests."

Austin hadn't shown up. I was disappointed. When I'd left the other day, I hoped that his confidence in jumping might have returned. But it looked like I'd been wrong. It seemed like he wasn't going to the event after all. My mission had failed.

I hadn't told anyone about my "lesson" with Austin. Matt and Reese had made a comment that morning when Austin hadn't appeared for gear check, but there had been no mention of him since.

Holding the reins in one hand, each of us bent our heads to check out the tests. I examined mine.

"Enter at rising trot," it read. "At X, halt. Salute the judge." It went on with instructions about trotting at certain letters, cantering in either direction, saluting the judge again, and walking out of the arena to finish.

"Does anyone have any questions?" Erica asked. Matt and Reese shook their heads.

"It's the same test as last year," said Reese.

I thought they both looked confident. Riding a dressage test was old news for them. I glanced at Jessica. If she had any concerns, she was keeping them quiet.

I had about a million questions. Where did the judges watch from? How did anyone know when it was their turn to ride? How did you know when to start the test?

But I didn't want to show my ignorance in front of the others by being the only one who didn't know.

I'll watch the others when we practice, I thought. *I can do whatever they do.*

Erica gave us all a few more minutes to memorize the test.

"All right, class," she said. "Everyone mount up. We'll start with you, Annie."

Terrified, I looked up from the test. "Reese can go first. Or Matt," I stuttered.

But Erica shook her head. "No. You go. I'll direct you if you need any help. Just circle your horse down at this end of the arena until I tell you to start. I'll be judging you as you go."

Oh well, I guess this is it, I thought.

I passed the paper to Reese and climbed onto Bobby's back. After a few circles Erica called, "You may begin the test now."

I asked Bobby to trot and steered him down the center of the arena. I tried to remember what had been written on the sheet.

At X, halt. Salute the judge.

I remembered seeing an X on the plan that I had printed off the riding club website.

I looked around frantically, trying to find the letter X among the painted letters that were attached on boards to the walls of the arena. Directly ahead of me was C, down the long sides were K, E, and H to the left and F, B, and M to the right.

I had almost ridden to C at the end of the arena when Erica stopped me.

"Annie, you didn't halt and salute at X," Erica said.

My face hot with embarrassment, I shot a quick glance at the others, who were all listening carefully.

"I'm sorry. I'm just a little nervous." My voice was so soft it could barely be heard.

Erica looked hard at me for a moment. "Annie," she explained gently. "X is an imaginary letter. It's in the middle of the arena between E and B. If you didn't know what to do, why didn't you ask?"

I stared quietly at the instructor, my eyes filling with tears. This was humiliating. I suddenly wanted more than anything to be back in the city hanging out with my old friend Jade, who didn't know one end of a horse from the other.

"Watch the others," Erica told me. Then she sent me back to the group.

Erica called on Reese to ride her test. I tried to watch Reese, then Matt, so I could learn from them. But my eyes were so misty that I couldn't seem to focus properly. I tried to listen, but all I could hear was a quiet roaring in my ears.

Later, I still felt horrible. I had wasted the lesson, and I still didn't know how to ride a dressage test.

What was the point in defying my father by riding if I couldn't even get through the first phase? In my imagination I could hear him telling me, "I told you so!"

The next time I showed up at the stables,
Erica wasn't around. I went straight to work.
After cleaning out all the stalls, I took a rake
and wheelbarrow in to pick up droppings.
Not long after I'd started working there, Erica
had explained that horses could get worms by
eating from dirty floors. The floors should be as
clean as our homes, she had said.

An hour later, I was halfway through
cleaning Erica's assortment of leather saddles
and bridles. As I worked, I considered my

options. I needed to think of another way to get Austin to the one-day event and somehow make it there myself without my father finding out. And with less than a week to go, I was running out of time.

Erica appeared in the doorway. "Annie, I'm glad you're still here," she said.

Erica was dressed in a clean shirt and neat jeans instead of her usual jodhpurs and riding vest. "If you have time when you're finished, come up to my house," she said. "I have a job for you." It was more of an order than an invitation. She left before I could answer.

When I was done working, I walked up the hill to Erica's house and knocked on the back door.

"Come in, Annie," Erica said, holding the door wide so that I could step into the small kitchen.

I looked around curiously. I could hear voices in another room, but then I realized it was the television.

A pile of dirty dishes clogged the sink. A pair of muddy riding boots had been flung into a corner, and there were books and papers all over the table.

I was shocked at the mess. Erica was so fussy about keeping the stables immaculate. I would have thought her house would be super clean, too.

Erica waved me into the living room. I'd been right about the television. I recognized the actors on the screen. The show was an old-fashioned crime series, one of my father's favorite shows.

"Have a seat," said Erica, pointing at the couch. I had to move an old jacket out of the way before settling myself on the old sofa.

"I just have to change," she told me. Then she disappeared into the back of the house.

I wasn't interested in the television show. I looked around the room. A remote control lay on a cluttered coffee table in the middle of the room. Next to the remote was a DVD with a hand-written label.

Curious, I leaned across and picked up the DVD. The writing was faded. I could barely read it.

Dressage with Majestic.

I had to squint to read, but I was pretty sure those were the words the label had written on it. I heard a door close. *It wouldn't hurt to check this out while Erica is changing,* I thought.

I slipped the disc into the DVD player on the top of the television. Then I picked up the remote control, found the play button, and carefully pushed it.

The screen went a little fuzzy, then cleared to show a girl entering a dressage arena on an elegant-looking black horse. I looked more closely and realized that the rider was Erica.

I leaned forward to see the horse better, but then jumped up guiltily when I heard Erica's voice.

"It's an old home movie," said Erica, appearing in the doorway. She was back to normal in jodhpurs, vest, and a faded t-shirt underneath.

"The horse's name was Majestic. He was very talented," Erica went on. She didn't seem at all upset that I had played the DVD while she was gone.

"What happened to him?" I wanted to know.

"I sold him for a good price." Then Erica shushed me with her finger and pointed to the screen. "Watch and listen," she said. We both sat down.

The next hour kept me absorbed as Erica played, paused, and rewound the DVD. She explained the movements and what she and her horse were being judged on in the test.

Here, in her own home, Erica was more relaxed than I had ever seen her. I found myself asking questions.

What was a diagonal? Erica explained that when trotting, the rider had to be rising in the suddle at the same time as the horse's outside leg was moving forward.

And canter leads? When the horse is on a circle, his inside front leg at the canter should be the leg that leads off first.

By the time the DVD was over, I knew I would never look as polished and refined as Majestic and Erica. I probably wouldn't remember to change my diagonals while trotting and check my canter leads. But at least I could try my first dressage test knowing the basics of what to do. Erica had saved me from making a total fool of myself.

Erica rose. She scanned the room, found her muddy riding boots, and put them on. I knew it was time to go. Then I suddenly remembered that Erica had brought me to the house to do a job.

I hesitated, feeling guilty that so much of my boss's time had been taken up by watching the DVD. "So what was the job?" I asked.

Erica looked at me for a moment, and then gave me a rare smile. "You just did it," she said. "Call it research, if you like."

I still didn't understand but Erica explained, "I brought you up here to show you the video. You did want to know how to ride a test, didn't you?"

I stared at Erica. I didn't know how to respond.

"Just consider it overtime," said Erica, laughing.

Chapter Ten

I came through the back door at my house to find my mother and Mrs. Moriarty sitting at the kitchen table. They had become good friends since we moved to Ridgeview.

I smelled coffee, and when I glanced at the table I saw two empty mugs and a crumb-covered plate with one last chocolate cookie remaining.

"Hello," I greeted the women. I leaned across my mother to reach the cookie.

"Great news!" Mom told me. She was smiling, but Mrs. Moriarty was watching me with a strange expression.

My father walked in from the living room. "Have you told her yet, Susan?" he asked. He sounded excited.

"Told me what?" I asked.

"I decided to let you enter the horse trials after all," my father said.

"You did? Dad, that's great!" I rushed toward him, wanting to throw my arms around him in a grateful hug. Up to now, my father had shown zero interest in my riding. *He must be finally coming around*, I thought.

"Yes, Ray Snyder was telling the manager from MC Developments that you had joined the riding club. His daughter is riding at the Willowvale event too. Mark thought it would be a good idea for me to meet him there. He has a property he wants to sell," Dad added. "We can talk business while we watch the two of you compete."

My smile faded. Business! It wasn't about me at all. As usual, my father's decision was all about what he wanted and had nothing to do with me. He seemed to think my feelings in the matter weren't important.

Despite the fact that I'd planned to go all along, and that now I really could, I was still mad about my father's selfishness.

Mrs. Moriarty rose from the table. "Well, thanks for the coffee, Susan. I should get home," she announced.

Then Mrs. Moriarty surprised me by shooting me a quick wink before heading for the back door. My mother got up and followed her out, chatting quietly. That left me alone with my father.

"We don't have a way for Bobby to get there. Remember, Dad?" I hoped my sarcasm was obvious.

"What's wrong now? I thought you wanted to go." My father looked baffled. "Besides, Mrs. Moriarty offered to take the horse."

I suddenly realized why Reese's mother had winked at me. As far as she had known, I had been going all along. She must not have said anything to my parents that gave me away. Thank goodness!

Even though now I was officially allowed to ride at the Willowvale event, I couldn't help feeling hurt. Why couldn't my dad be interested in me for my own sake?

I thought about the man from MC Developments and his daughter. I felt an angry stab of dislike for both of them. But right at that moment, I liked my own father even less.

* * *

The sign had a big red arrow pointing to the left. "Willowvale Horse Trials this way," it read.

I sat in the back of my father's car behind both of my parents. We were following Reese and Mrs. Moriarty, who had the two horses in the trailer behind her SUV.

Mrs. Moriarty's SUV turned off the road and eased over a bumpy trail. Thick bushes hugged each side of the trail. They made it impossible to see more than a few feet beyond the car windows.

The Moriartys stopped in front of an old farm gate. Reese jumped out to open it. From my seat in the back of my parents' car, I craned my neck to see into the trailer and check on the horses. All I could see were two round rumps and the tops of the animals' heads.

I saw Jefferson's eyes, his white muzzle, and his two gray ears that stuck up like a portable TV antenna. The rest of him, I knew, was covered from head to tail by a fancy tartan blanket and hood.

Bobby's outfit was much less impressive. An old cotton blanket, covered in patches, wasn't much decoration for my beautiful chestnut horse, but it was the best I could do for him. Reese had far more expensive accessories for her horse.

At home, Bobby didn't wear a blanket at all. But Mrs. Moriarty had seemed to think he needed one. She'd offered me one of Jefferson's old blankets when she had arrived to pick Bobby up at six that morning.

"You should use it," Reese's mother had said. "It's our third spare."

Reese waited until both vehicles were through the gate, then closed it.

This is it, I thought. I hoped that Austin had changed his mind and decided to come.

He has to be here, I thought. *He just has to be.*

I breathed in sharply at the sight that
opened up before us. The Willowvale Horse
Club grounds were in an enormous open
paddock. The ground was mostly flat, with a
few gentle slopes.

The place was busy. Horses were
everywhere. Riders in different riding club
uniforms warmed up before the event. There
was a large clubhouse to the right of us.
Several people were unloading show-jumping
equipment from a trailer. They were setting up

jumps on a flat grassy area that was roped off with colored flags.

On the left were the dressage arenas. Each one was carefully measured out and surrounded by a rope boundary. On the outside of each arena were little metal stands with letters painted on them.

"Wow," said my father, sounding slightly awed. "Who would have thought there'd be so many horse lovers?"

My mother murmured something that I didn't catch. I ignored them and kept quiet, taking it all in.

The most impressive thing was the cross-country course. I knew what it was right away because of the fences of various shapes and sizes that dotted the paddock.

There were people all over the course. By the numbers that many of them wore, I could tell they were competitors, walking the course and checking out the route they would later ride. Each fence was marked by numbers and flags — a red flag on one end, a white flag on the other.

The overall effect of flags, horses, and riders together made a startling blur of color and movement.

Reese's mother pulled the car and trailer into a parking spot. Dad pulled in behind the trailer.

"Dad!" I yelled at him. "You can't park there. We have to unload."

"Oh, of course," my father said gruffly. His face turned red behind his beard as he quickly backed up the car and re-parked it beside Mrs. Moriarty's. Reese and I stepped out to unload the horses. Reese's mother began sorting through tack and grooming gear in the back of her car.

My parents stood around awkwardly. *They look so out of place*, I thought. I wished they hadn't come.

"Hey, Dad, why don't you go look around while we get ready? Maybe you'll find your friend," I said sourly.

"Good idea!" My father seemed relieved at this suggestion.

"What time are you riding, Annie?" my mother asked.

"My dressage test is at ten," I said.

"We'll be there to watch you," my mother promised.

My parents wandered off. I couldn't help but smile as I watched them trying to avoid a pile of manure that was in their path. They were definitely city people. Buying a country property and raising sheep hadn't changed that.

For the next forty minutes, I followed Reese's lead. We got our horses ready. It was just like getting ready for a rally, except that I felt even more nervous.

Reese's mother had suddenly turned hyper. The first thing she did was carefully braid Jefferson's mane into a line of tight little knobs up his neck. Then she started on his tail, working the gray mess of hair into a neat braid at the top.

I looked at the braids jealously. With Bobby's thick mane, I had no idea where to start. I wasn't very good at braiding anyway. Bobby's thick, slightly messy mane would just have to be okay the way it was.

Reese didn't seem at all impressed by her mother's work when Jefferson's hair was done. I felt like my friend just took her mother's help for granted. I smiled, trying to imagine my own mother braiding Bobby's mane. The image was pretty funny. She wouldn't even know where to start.

I buckled my helmet under my chin. My body shook with nervousness. I was having trouble believing I was finally here. It was like a dream come true.

When we were ready, Mrs. Moriarty looked carefully at Reese, making sure that her hair was tied back neatly and picking imaginary pieces of fluff off her sweater.

"Leave me alone, Mom," Reese snapped. "I can dress myself, you know."

"You need to impress the judges," Mrs. Moriarty told her daughter. "It could give you an extra mark or two."

"Mom," Reese whined, "the judges are marking my horse and my riding. It's not a fashion show! Come on, Annie, let's get over to gear check and then start warming up." Reese trotted away, and I quickly nudged Bobby to catch up.

I couldn't remember seeing so much activity in one place since I left the city. Everyone was so busy. People were warming up, doing a last-minute read-through of their dressage tests, or walking their jumping courses.

Occasionally there would be a burst of noise from the public address system. The announcements were mostly for competitors, calling them to appear at one of the rings for their dressage tests or a jumping round.

By the time I was due to start my dressage test, I felt sick and my hands were clammy.

As I rode up to the judge, I spotted my parents. They were standing to the left of the roped-off arena. My father was deep in conversation with a man I didn't know. *That must be the manager,* I thought bitterly.

I looked away, blocking all thoughts but my dressage test, which I repeated over and over in my head.

After telling the judge my name, I trotted a circle outside the dressage arena, waiting for the judge to wave me in and start the test. As I circled, I had trouble holding the reins. They'd gotten slippery from my sweaty, trembling hands.

My life had changed so much in the time since I moved to Ridgeview. Learning to ride was like opening a door and finding a fantastic gift inside.

It was mostly really fun. But it seemed like every time I found a gift, there was another one inside the wrapping, challenging me to unwrap the mystery.

The more I discovered, the more there was to be discovered. Sometimes it was all a little overwhelming.

As I directed Bobby through the narrow opening and into the arena, I made a decision. No matter what happened today, I would finish the event. I would not let my nerves ruin things.

Then I rode my test.

Chapter Twelve

I came out of the arena and saw Reese and Matt clapping.

I exhaled a long, relieved breath. The first phase was over, and to my very great surprise, I had actually ridden the whole thing without forgetting what to do or otherwise screwing things up.

Reese was the first to congratulate me. "Good test. Not bad for your first time."

"Nice job, Annie," Matt said, smiling.

"Do you think so? Really?" I asked nervously. "I'm just glad it's over. How did you two do?"

"My test was okay, I think," said Reese, with quiet confidence. "We won't really know until the scores are posted later."

Matt just shrugged and laughed. "Dressage is not my strong point," he said. "But just wait for the cross country." Matt rubbed Bullet's neck affectionately. "We'll fly through, won't we, buddy?"

My parents walked up then. "That looked good," my mother told me.

My father was still in business mode. "So what happens now?" he wanted to know. He glanced at the watch on his wrist. "What time does this thing end, anyway?"

"It won't be over until late, Mr. Boyd," said Reese. "There are four ratings to get through.

The dressage usually takes forever. There's show jumping and cross country, and then we all have to wait for the final scores to see where we place."

"Hmmm," said Dad. "I guess I better go find Mark. See you later, Annie." Then my parents left.

Matt's talk of jumping had made my stomach flip. I glanced around. "Where's Jessica?" I asked. "And has anybody seen Austin?"

"Nope, haven't seen Austin. But Jessica's in there," Matt said. He pointed to the same ring that I had ridden in.

Jessica was riding her test. I stared.

Ripple's mane and tail were braided like Jefferson's, and her coat shone like black satin. The little horse moved beautifully, and Jessica looked perfect.

I whimpered. "Help. How can I compete with that?"

Reese chuckled. "Hey," she said, "don't bet on anything. For D rating, Jessica's dressage is good. It comes from all that show practice. But just wait and see how they do with the jumping."

Back at the trailer, Reese and I unsaddled and got ready to walk the cross-country course. Then a name we recognized was called over the loudspeaker. "Austin Ryan," a man's voice called. "Austin Ryan, please come to the B rating dressage ring."

Relief surged through me. "Austin's here!" I announced unnecessarily to Reese.

"I thought Matt said he wasn't coming," Reese said.

"Must have changed his mind," I said happily.

I checked my watch. I was due to ride my cross-country course in an hour, with show jumping right away afterward. I would have liked to return to the dressage rings and see for myself if Austin had shown up to compete, but there was no time.

Walking the jumping courses made me nervous all over again. On the cross-country course there was a narrow ditch that looked particularly scary. There was also a brick wall that, although quite low, looked very solid. I couldn't help but think of the disaster that would happen if I fell and landed on it.

The show jumps, too, looked challenging. I hoped Bobby wouldn't spook at the brightly painted poles and boards.

Even though the jumps were all numbered, I wasn't sure I'd be able to remember the order. I made a point of walking through the course twice.

After we finished walking the jumping course, Reese dragged me across to the clubhouse to check the dressage scores. Each group's scores were written on sheets of paper, which were pinned to a board on the wall.

Reese's finger followed the list of names in C rating until she found her own.

"Hey, look," she cried excitedly. "I placed sixth so far. And Matt is doing really well too."

"Congratulations," I said, giving Reese a quick hug. "Does that mean you'll get a ribbon?"

Reese laughed. "No way. We still have the jumping, and anything could happen. If I go clear and someone ahead of me doesn't, I could go up, but if I knock a rail or have a refusal, I could go down just as easily. Matt still has a chance. He and Bullet usually jump clear." Reese scanned the board. "Your scores aren't up yet."

I spotted a sheet with "B Rating Dressage" typed across the top. "Let's see how Austin did," I said, checking the sheet. "Here's his name. He must be here somewhere, then."

I stood on my tiptoes and looked around, trying to find Austin. But, with so many people everywhere, I had no hope of seeing him.

I turned my attention back to the board. "Reese, what does this score mean?" I asked. Austin had a score of 25, which meant nothing to me.

But Reese whistled. "Hey, he's in first place," she said. "If he jumps clean, he'll win."

A man's voice on the loudspeaker informed us that the B rating cross-country phase was about to begin.

"Come on," said Reese, grabbing my arm. "We'll have just enough time to watch Austin's round before we have to saddle up again."

I wanted to watch Austin jump the cross-country, but I held back.

What if something went wrong? If I saw Austin having a problem, I would never have the courage to ride the rest of the event myself!

"No!" I said. "Let's just go and get ready. I'm nervous enough as it is without watching anybody else."

Reese shook her head. "What are you worried about? It's only D rating," she said. "Bobby could probably do the whole thing with his eyes shut!"

Bobby probably could, I thought, *but he has a major burden to carry — me.*

My legs trembled as I walked Bobby into the
cross-country starting area. A couple of practice
jumps had been set up near the start box, and
several riders were tackling them. Others quietly
walked or trotted around, waiting their turn to
be called.

*I don't have to go through with this. I could
quit the event*, I thought, as I desperately tried to
calm myself down. *Who would care? No one would
even know.*

I knew my dad would care. He'd be mortified if I chickened out in front of everyone. I hadn't seen my parents for a while. My father had mumbled something about finding Mark.

He's probably busy watching Mark's kid ride, I thought resentfully. *Probably telling Mark how great Mark's kid is. Meanwhile, here I am.*

There was a rider entering the starting box. A man checked his watch. "Thirty seconds to go," he told the rider.

I couldn't help but admire the rider's outfit. Whoever the girl was, she had changed out of the sweater and tie that everyone wore for the dressage test. This rider now wore a brightly colored silk top and matching helmet cover. She looked amazing.

"Ten seconds," the man announced. He began counting down. It was only when the rider left the box in a slow canter that I recognized the horse.

It was Ripple. The girl in the fancy silk clothes was Jessica!

I watched Jessica go through the first part of the course. Ripple cleanly completed the first two obstacles, a wide log and some low drums. Jessica kept the horse in a steady rhythm. I had to admit the pair looked very professional.

My attention was drawn back to the man with the watch. He seemed to be searching for something. I wondered what or who he was looking for.

"Number 32," an angry voice crackled in my ear. The man was speaking to me. "Number 32! Aren't you number 32?"

"Oh, yes . . . that's me," I stuttered.

"You've got thirty seconds."

Gulping, I tightened my grip on the reins and walked Bobby into the box. Everything seemed to stop as I listened to the countdown.

"... 8, 7, 6, 5, 4, 3, 2, 1, go!"

It did seem like Bobby knew what he was doing. He left the box in a loping canter. But I needed to feel like I was in control. I reined him back to a fast trot. His ears were pricked, and there was an eager bounce to his strides as he covered the ground.

I twisted my fingers into his mane and looked toward the first jump on the course. Bobby floated over it and traveled on.

"One," I counted and focused on the next jump. Below me, Bobby's hooves beat out a muffled tempo on the short summer grass. A faint breeze caressed my neck beneath my helmet.

After the second jump, Bobby once again broke into a canter. This time, I allowed him to stretch out a little. As he cantered, I could feel myself smiling.

The butterflies were gone. The other competitors were gone. I felt suspended in time. There was nothing but the warm, slick sweat that was beginning to form on my horse's neck . . . the thrill and freedom of running.

We soared over jump number three, then four, five! More than ever before, I felt a connection with Bobby, a sense of partnership. It was amazing.

There was a long stretch of ground to cover before jump six. That was that scary ditch. Ahead of me, I could see a stopped rider.

It was Jessica. Ripple, with her feet planted stubbornly, was refusing to go over the ditch. I wanted a clear run at the jump. I slowed Bobby back to a trot, trying to give Jessica some time.

Jessica yelled, "Jump!"

But Ripple wasn't listening. Wide-eyed, the horse stared at the hole in the ground as if there might have been some ferocious, horse-eating monster lurking inside.

Bobby and I were almost there. I didn't know what to do. Was I supposed to wait until Jessica went over? Or was Jessica supposed to get out of the way and let me pass?

The jump judge, a man wearing a canvas sunhat, sat in a chair off to one side of the jump. There was a judge at each jump to record the riders' penalties, I remembered. He stood up and started speaking to Jessica. I could see that Jessica was arguing with him.

I was about to rein Bobby back to a walk when I heard the grim-faced man growl something and point sharply in the direction of the start box. Was he . . . ? Yes!

Jessica, with a scowl on her face, turned Ripple around. They headed away from the jump.

I felt a stab of pity for Jessica. It looked as if she had been eliminated, and at her first one-day event!

But there was no time to think about that. The way was now clear. I urged Bobby on and over the ditch, breathing a sigh of relief as we landed and Bobby cantered on.

I was panting harder than my horse by the time I cantered triumphantly through the finish flags. I hadn't realized until now that most of the way around I'd been holding my breath.

After I was done, I rode Bobby into the vet check area. All of the horses had to have their heart rate checked after the cross-country phase. That was to make sure they hadn't been hurt by the run.

In the vet check area, an official instructed me to dismount and loosen my horse's girth.

I praised Bobby. I hugged his sweaty head in my hands and planted a kiss on the end of his muzzle.

"You were amazing, boy!" I told the horse breathlessly. "That was wonderful, Bobby!"

"I guess you're pretty happy with yourself," a girl said. I turned to find Jessica, with Ripple, glaring at me.

"What do you mean?" I asked, confused by the other girl's accusing tone.

Jessica laughed. "You know exactly what I mean. You had me eliminated." She pointed her finger at me. I stepped back.

"No. I didn't," I said. "The jump judge sent you off."

But Jessica wasn't listening. "I was winning!" she shouted. "It's your fault I was eliminated."

I stared at her in disbelief.

The angry girl marched out of the vet check area, dragging a tired Ripple along behind her. Just then Matt and Reese rode by. They were heading for the start box. The C-rating cross-country phase was about to start.

"Hey," Reese called, "did you make it?"

I grinned shyly. "I did," I answered. Then I wrapped my arms around Bobby's neck. "We did," I added.

"Congratulations," Matt and Reese said.

"Not bad for a first-timer," added Matt.

I grinned. I was feeling pretty good about myself at that moment. "Thanks. And good luck to both of you, too."

Then I turned back to Bobby.

Phase three. Show jumping. I tried to memorize my course and calm down. Even though I'd done well on the cross-country course, I knew I wasn't finished yet. The warm-up area was crowded with riders. The other phases were finished, and everyone seemed to be here. If I messed this up now, there would be dozens of people watching.

Matt and Reese were there. They had both made it through their cross-country test.

Reese had told me that Matt had gotten in trouble for riding his horse too fast. A judge had yelled at him.

Matt then told me that Reese had almost missed a jump. She'd screwed up at the last moment and had to do some sharp turns to get Jefferson back on the right line.

Now they stood holding their horses. It wasn't worth unsaddling when it was their turn right after the D-rating riders.

Jessica was nowhere to be seen.

Reese must have noticed me scanning the other riders. "Don't waste your time looking for Jessica," she said. "She gave up and went home. I heard it was all your fault."

I frowned, but Reese laughed. "Don't worry," said Reese. "We don't believe her. Jessica has a problem with accepting responsibility. Everyone knows that."

But the truth was, I wasn't looking for Jessica. "Have you seen Austin yet?" I asked.

Reese shrugged. "He's around somewhere. There was a cross-country score on the board for him. He did well. All he has to do is make it through the show jumping and he'll win. Look, there he is!"

Reese pointed. Austin and Cruise were entering the ring to begin their show jump round. The B-rating jumps looked high — much higher than the ones I would be attempting. Reese, Matt, and I fell silent to watch.

We watched Austin approach the judge. When a bell rang, signaling him to begin his round, his horse began to trot a circle around the course.

Austin frowned in concentration as he rode up to the first obstacle. Cruise went in crookedly, and there was a clunk of hoof on wood as the horse's feet tapped the rail. The rail rattled in the cup, but it didn't fall — no penalty.

I stared, mesmerized. "Come on, Austin," I whispered. "You can do this."

Next was a double fence, then a spread. Austin seemed to have settled into a rhythm. With each jump they cleared, his stance seemed to become more confident.

Six more jumps. One at a time, Austin and Cruise jumped over them. Austin finished the course. The spectators clapped and cheered loudly.

Matt whistled, Reese clapped. I began breathing again. I looked over my jumps course again and felt a little less anxious. Austin had done it. I could too.

My parents walked up. Both of them carried steaming cups of coffee. My father looked mad.

I guessed he was probably getting bored. This wasn't really his scene.

"Where's your friend?" I asked, trying to talk about something my father was interested in. My father didn't reply. He just glared at me.

"Robert!" Mom said. "It's not Annie's fault."

My father's jaw tightened, but he didn't say anything.

"What's not my fault?" I asked, frowning at my mom.

"Mark Coulson's daughter was eliminated from the competition," Mom explained. "For some reason they seem to think it was your fault. But that's totally ridiculous. I saw what happened. You were nowhere near her."

I stared at my mother. It took a few moments for her words to sink in.

Mark Coulson!

I was stunned. Dad's client was Jessica's father.

Reese and Matt had been silent, but now they both burst out laughing.

Annoyed, Dad turned to them. "And what is it that you two think is so amusing?"

I was pleased to see that Matt didn't seem at all afraid of my dad. "Oh, it's just Jessica Coulson," he explained. "She's so incredibly spoiled. She probably told her dad it was Annie's fault, and he fell for it. Annie had nothing to do with it."

Dad didn't look convinced, but he didn't say anything else.

"I better go warm up," I said, cutting the conversation short.

I took Bobby over a couple of warm-up jumps and tried to calm myself down.

I heard my name being called from the side of the warm-up area. I turned to see Austin. He was on foot, holding Cruise by the reins.

"Congratulations," I told him.

"Thanks. I almost didn't come," said Austin. "I really wasn't scared, you know," he added. "That's what everybody thinks, but it wasn't that."

I frowned. "We didn't . . . " I began.

But Austin interrupted me. "I know I acted like a brat when I fell that day at the riding club," he said. "I was embarrassed that I fell off in front of Penelope. I guess I was showing off." Austin looked down at the ground. "Now she probably thinks I'm a total loser."

"You're not a loser, Austin. You're the best rider I know," I told him.

"I am?" Austin asked. He sounded surprised.

"You are." I glanced up to see the gate marshal waving in my direction. Suddenly, I knew I could do this. No sweat.

"I'm next," I told Austin. "Wish me luck." I turned Bobby toward the gate.

"Go for it!" Austin yelled at the top of his voice.

Bobby and I entered the ring and approached the judging tent. The judge was a silver-haired old man with a bushy mustache. A young girl with a clipboard was sitting next to him.

"What's your name?" the judge asked me.

"Annie Boyd," I said.

The girl with the clipboard wrote something down.

"And your horse's name?" the judge asked.

"Bobby."

The judge nodded. As he picked up the starting bell, he added with a kind smile, "Good luck, and don't forget to have fun out there, Annie."

I flashed him a brief, nervous smile before turning my attention to the course. I heard the bell ring and looked ahead to the start flags.

Bobby was a little too eager. He rushed at the first jump, which worried me, but managed to clear it okay. The second and third jumps had been placed in a straight line, just a few strides apart.

I played it safe, slowing Bobby down a little as I turned him for the approach. Bobby popped over one, then two, perfectly.

Just as before in the cross-country phase, I suddenly forgot to be nervous. Energy rushed through me. Bobby picked up the pace just a little.

I rode the rest of the course as if in a dream, only coming back to reality as I passed through the finish flags to a burst of applause from the onlookers.

* * *

"I have the great pleasure of introducing a special guest to present the ribbons." The president of Willowvale Horse Club was speaking. She was a short, plump lady with gray hair.

She looks like someone's grandmother, I thought.

The horses were all happily munching hay, tied up near the trailers. They were blissfully unaware of what was happening outside the club room. I wished I was as unaware as Bobby.

I stood with my parents, Mrs. Moriarty and Reese, Matt and the Snyders, and Austin, who had finally joined up with the rest of the

Ridgeview crowd.

The results for B rating had been posted. Everybody knew Austin had won. Modestly, but with an air of quiet pride, Austin had accepted the handshakes and congratulations.

The president clasped her hands and continued with her announcement. "Everyone, please welcome Penelope O'Reilly!" she said. Everybody clapped.

Starting with the winner, Penelope announced each rider's name and presented them with a lovely wide satin sash. When it came to Austin's turn, Penelope took a moment longer to speak with him. I couldn't hear what she was saying, but Reese and I exchanged a knowing look.

He's back on track, I thought with satisfaction.

I couldn't help thinking that maybe, in a

small way, I'd had something to do with that.

Reese had also placed. She accepted her white fourth-place ribbon happily. Mrs. Moriarty congratulated her daughter. Then she said, "You really should have tried a little harder in the dressage test, honey."

Reese rolled her eyes, but I could tell she was a little hurt.

It made me think. I had been feeling a little jealous of Reese and the way her mom was so interested in her riding. But now, I thought that maybe it was better to be able to do things at your own pace instead of having someone constantly pushing you to do better all the time.

Matt had been eliminated from the competition when he and Bullet had knocked a rail down in the show jumping. He didn't seem too concerned.

I had the feeling that Matt only came for the cross country and the chance to ride fast over jumps.

I hadn't even bothered to check the scores. Even though I had gone clear, I felt I must have lost time in the cross-country, since I had trotted a lot of it.

My dressage wasn't that great either, I knew. I didn't mind. I was happy to watch the others receive their prizes. My first event had gone way better than I'd expected. That was enough.

I glanced at my father. He still looked grumpy. I felt a little sorry for him. It would probably take him quite a bit of work to get Mark Coulson back on his side again.

Penelope started on the D-rating ribbons. She read out each winner's name, presenting a different-colored sash for each placing: blue for first, then red, yellow, white, pink . . .

Suddenly, everyone was pushing me forward.

My mother let out a gasp of pleased surprise. "Good job, honey," Mom said.

I didn't fully understand what was happening until Penelope was handing me a green ribbon and congratulating me. I couldn't believe it. In my very first competition, I had finished in sixth place!

I looked at my father. He'd thought I'd fall off, but I hadn't.

I did pretty well for a beginner, I thought proudly.

Back at the trailer, I draped the sash around Bobby's neck. "You won this, Bobby. You carried me through," I told the horse.

But Reese frowned. "Hey," she protested. "You had to ride him, you know. He doesn't come with a remote control!"

Mom held up a camera. "Smile," she ordered.

"Come on, Bobby," I said, wrapping my arms around the horse. "You smile too!"

In the moment it took for the flash to pop in our faces, everyone else melted away. There was just me and Bobby — partners.

About the Author

When she was growing up, Bernadette Kelly desperately wanted her own horse. Although she rode other people's horses, she didn't get one of her own until she was an adult. Many years later, she is still obsessed with horses. Luckily, she lives in the country, where there is plenty of room for her four-legged friends. When she's not writing or working with her horses, Bernadette and her daughter compete in riding club competitions.

Horse Tips from Bernadette

⊙ A horse has a mind of its own and can react in unpredictable ways. A horse is NOT a machine. It can think and feel and needs to be treated with kindness and respect.

⊙ The best and safest way to learn to ride is under the guidance of a qualified instructor.

⊙ Learning to be safe around horses is a must.

⊙ Learn everything you can about horses.

For more, visit Bernadette's website at
www.bernadettekelly.com.au/horses

Glossary

- **accurately** (AK-yuh-ruht-lee)—correctly

- **ambitions** (am-BISH-uhnz)—goals

- **canter** (KAN-tur)—to move at a speed between a gallop and a trot

- **category** (KAT-uh-gor-ee)—group

- **confident** (KON-fuh-duhnt)—having a strong belief in your own abilities

- **determination** (di-tur-min-AY-shuhn)—having made a firm decision to do something

- **dressage** (dress-AHJ)—a method of riding and training a horse to perform

- **eliminate** (i-LIM-uh-nate)—to get rid of

- **jodhpurs** (JOD-purz)—pants worn for horseback riding

- **obstacle** (OB-stuh-kuhl)—something in the way

- **paddock** (PAD-uck)—an enclosed area where horses can graze or exercise

- **salute** (suh-LOOT)—to raise your right hand to your forehead

- **tack** (TAK)—equipment that you need to ride a horse

Advice from Annie

Dear Annie,

I hate to admit it, but I'm afraid of trying new things. My biggest fear is trying something and being terrible at it. I hate messing up, especially in front of other people. I'm afraid everyone will laugh at me. What can I do to get over my fears?

Scared in Seattle

Dear Scared in Seattle,

It's a good thing that you've realized that this is a problem. Understanding that you're afraid of new experiences is the first step to making that fear go away!

Here's how to be brave!

1. **Try things.** You can't get over this fear unless you try. Make a list of new things you'd like to learn or try. Your list can include everyday things, like learning how to do a layup or joining a band, and more difficult things, like learning how to speak Russian or writing a novel.

2. **Set goals.** Look at your list, and give each new thing a goal date. Maybe you'd like to learn how to do a layup this month, but you'll be happy if you write a novel by 2030.

3. **Try again.** If you screw up, even if it's in front of other people, just try again. You can't learn anything without trying!

4. **Get over other people.** Accept that you're not perfect, but you're great anyway.

Good luck! Remember, trying and failing is the first step of being great at something.

Love,
♡ Annie

The Ridgeview Book Club Discussion Guide

Use these reading group questions when you and your friends discuss this book.

1. Annie and her father don't seem to get along. Talk about getting along with parents. Is it important to you or not? Explain your answer. What could Annie do to improve her relationship with her dad? What could Annie's dad do to improve his relationship with his daughter?

2. How does Annie get the confidence to go through with the one-day event? What about Austin? Why do you think he finally decided to go through with the event?

3. Talk about Jessica Coulson. How does she treat people? How do people feel about her? Why did Jessica blame her elimination on Annie? What other effects did her accusation have?

The Ridgeview Book Club Journal Prompts

A journal is a private place to record your thoughts and ideas. Use these prompts to get started. If you like, share your writing with your friends.

1. Write about a time you tried something even though you were afraid. What were you afraid of? What was the result? How did you feel afterward?

2. Everyone in the world has to ask for help sometimes. Write about a time you needed help. Who did you go to for help? What help did you need? What ended up happening? Were you happy with the result?

3. Do you belong to a team or have a group of friends who share a common interest? Choose one friend or teammate to write about. Why is that person a good friend or teammate? What have you learned from her or him? What have you helped him or her learn?

Join the Ridgeview Riding Club!

Read all of Annie's adventures.